Angela

PRAISE FOR *STORYSHARES*

"One of the brightest innovators and game-changers in the education industry."
– Forbes

"Your success in applying research-validated practices to promote literacy serves as a valuable model for other organizations seeking to create evidence-based literacy programs."

- Library of Congress

"We need powerful social and educational innovation, and Storyshares is breaking new ground. The organization addresses critical problems facing our students and teachers. I am excited about the strategies it brings to the collective work of making sure every student has an equal chance in life."
– Teach For America

"Around the world, this is one of the up-and-coming trailblazers changing the landscape of literacy and education."
- International Literacy Association

"It's the perfect idea. There's really nothing like this. I mean wow, this will be a wonderful experience for young people."   - Andrea Davis Pinkney, Executive Director, Scholastic

"Reading for meaning opens opportunities for a lifetime of learning. Providing emerging readers with engaging texts that are designed to offer both challenges and support for each individual will improve their lives for years to come. Storyshares is a wonderful start."
- David Rose, Co-founder of CAST & UDL

Angela

Caroline Gee

STORYSHARES

Story Share, Inc.
New York. Boston. Philadelphia

Storyshares
Story Share, Inc.
24 N. Bryn Mawr Avenue #340
Bryn Mawr, PA 19010-3304
www.storyshares.org

Inspiring reading with a new kind of book.

Interest Level: High School
Grade Level Equivalent: 3.6

9781642614633

Book design by Storyshares

Printed in the United States of America

Storyshares Presents

1

It started because somebody wanted a tuna sandwich.

In our tiny but neat living room, Charlie spread out on the sofa and sighed dramatically. "I'm so hungry," she said. "I haven't eaten since last night."

Judy and Becky gasped in unison — and also in admiration. Charlie was one of those limelight-loving kids with parents who were so hipster, they decided to give their daughter a boy's name. Patting her stomach, if you could even call it a stomach, Charlie demanded a sandwich.

"I have turkey," I offered.

"No, no. I don't eat meat. Do you have tuna?" she asked.

So there I was, two minutes later, at the doorway to the even smaller kitchen. The girls' fast-paced chatter, despite being only two yards behind me, seemed to fade away. Instead, the kitchen's dingy white walls and oak brown cupboards pressed intensely into my vision. Oh, gosh, the kitchen. Ma wouldn't be home for another two hours. It should be okay, right?

Like a mouse, I scampered into the kitchen. No time to waste — where was the bread? Pulling the week-old loaf from the cabinet, I scrounged around in the cupboard for the tuna. *Tuna, tuna, tuna*, rang insistently in my head.

Small grey tin in my hand, I then reached for the utensils cabinet. Knife out, perfect. Plate out, perfect. Time to assemble.

I got as far as placing the two slices of bread on the porcelain plate. Then she appeared.

"What are you doing?"

It was my fault for not paying closer attention. Usually the neat click of the front door and the jangle of keys alerted me to her presence. If not that, I should have noticed when my classmates' gossip came to an abrupt stop. Instead, the wiry form of her, my mother, sprang into the doorframe and seemed to grow into a colossal giant.

"What are you doing?" she asked again.

"Uh..." I said, attempting to hide the sandwich ensemble from Ma with my body.

It was no use.

"Why are you in my kitchen?" she demanded. Her drawn-in eyebrows squiggled up and down aggressively. Then her face scrunched into its familiar, hawk-like glare. "Out! You're ruining everything!"

If Charlie, Judy, and Becky were hoping for some drama, they got it. It wasn't my intention to put on a show, but fifteen straight minutes of my mother ranting in her shrill, piercing voice certainly made a mark. After gaping at my mom's increasingly red face, the girls finally had the sense to leave. But not before giving me visibly annoyed looks.

What? I wanted to shout back. *It's not my fault I have a psycho mom.*

The rest of the night didn't improve very much. Dad was late returning from work which, of course, made Ma angry. I could practically see flames rising from her flushed cheeks.

"You aren't supposed to go into my kitchen!" she spat in Mandarin.

"I'm sorry, Ma," I murmured. It wasn't safe for me to speak at a normal volume yet.

Sorry wasn't enough. Nothing would be enough. While sweeping all four corners of our cramped apartment, Mom continued to rant.

About the kitchen. About her job at the library. About the ungrateful kids who asked too many questions. About the people who checked out too many books. About the tuna smell that was stinking up the kitchen.

Only when she began cooking dinner — bland chicken broth with ramen noodles and bok choy — did she fall silent. Food, no matter how plain it may be, always improved my mom's mood. Just as she set out hot steaming bowls of chewy noodles bouncing in clear broth, the familiar sigh of dad's voice sounded from the front door.

He hobbled in, limping from his left leg as usual. Placing his bag on the sofa, Dad sank into his worn-out chair and pulled the noodles toward him.

"How was work, Dad?" I asked.

"Busy," he responded.

And that was that. It wasn't that my dad was grumpy or curt. He was just dog-worn tired, and I could see it in every crease of his face.

We ate in silence for ten minutes. Only after slurping up every last drop of the soup did Dad raise his head and drop the bomb.

2

"I got laid off."

"What?" Mom snapped, her face suddenly red.

"The company isn't doing too well—"

"You said this job was stable!"

"I know, but my boss won't tell me anything—"

"Why can't you just hold a job? You're pathetic. I should just kick you out on the street now."

Dad just took it, not even bothering to defend himself. He just sat there, content and full, having grown an impenetrable skin against the barbs of Ma's insults long ago.

I didn't say anything either. Honestly, I was just glad that Ma's stinging rant wasn't against me for once. But I knew exactly what would happen from here. It was time to move.

Even if I didn't want to, it didn't matter. In this household, I was clay; mashed, squished, and pressed by my dad's endless search to find work and my mom's nasty mood swings.

Maybe it would be a good thing. By now, the whole school had probably heard from Charlie about that Chinese girl's crazy mom.

"It must be because they're Chinese," kids would say.

And they would all give me sidelong glances as I passed in the hall, acting as if my short black hair and sensible glasses were anything but normal in their privileged lives.

For all the times when moving felt like a disaster, there were times when moving was a rare blessing.

We ended up moving four more times in the next year.

From Woodbridge to Winnipeg, then to Toronto, then to Vancouver, and finally back to Toronto. By this time, I was entering my sophomore year of high school. My freshman year had been so choppy that I felt like I had accumulated what couldn't be more than one month of quality academics.

In Toronto, we settled into one of the many red-brick tract houses in Richmond Hill. The location wasn't bad. We were across from a small forest, with a winding trail that led to an elementary school. I would spend hours swinging from the creaky swing set at that school, waiting for the sun to set and cherishing each minute I didn't have to be at home.

Often, I felt like I was waiting for something. What that was, I had no idea.

Angela

3

The doors opened. A sea of foreign faces. I was the lone fish in a sea of cliques and squads. Looking around, I gulped hard. I was the only Asian.

Clarity High School was possibly the most predominantly Caucasian high school I had stepped foot into so far. Usually, the schools had some African Americans, Mexicans, or even the rare Asian mixed in. Once, I met an Arabic person. But here? Every face that turned towards me with either a smile or raised eyebrow was white.

So, this was going well.

Angela

The first few classes were a blur. I sat alone, yet was constantly surrounded by throngs of people. Each teacher introduced me — "Everyone, this is Angela!" — and I would attempt a small wave and a smile.

Students' eyes seemed to drill into me, into my too-pale skin and my nonexistent eyes. Some girls threw amused looks in my direction. I noticed many of them had those popular shoes, the ones with white stripes on the sides. Those same girls sported skin-tight tank tops and matching jewelry, all of which Ma would never have allowed me to wear.

In my last class of the day, pre-calculus, I finally made real human contact. Out of the corner of my eye, I noticed a girl slide into the seat next to me. She was gorgeous, with silky blonde hair and bright blue eyes. Then, lo and behold, she tapped on my shoulder.

"Hey! You're new here, right?" she asked cheerfully.

"Oh, uh, yeah. I just moved here," I responded, taken aback. Someone was actually talking to me!

"What's your name? I'm Laura."

"I'm Angela. Nice to meet you." I smiled weakly at Laura, who for some reason was beaming at me. Turning back to my planner, I doodled on the paper, not knowing what to do.

"Watch out for the Sistas."

"Huh?" I looked up.

Laura repeated, "The Sistas. They all coordinate their outfits every day. I think today is skirt day."

She nodded toward a girl a few seats away, and I recognized her from my English class. She had glossy brown hair, as if straight from Teen Vogue. She was completely absorbed with her phone.

"I think I saw some girls wearing matching skirts," I said. "What's so bad about them?"

Laura's jaw dropped. "What's so bad about them?" she squawked. "Oh gosh, they are absolutely awful people. Snarky, self-obsessed, think that they're better than everyone else."

"Oh." I nodded sympathetically.

There were girls like "the Sistas" at every school I had attended. Usually, they didn't pay me much attention. I wasn't worth their time.

At that moment, the teacher started class. Calculus had always come easy to me, so I had time to think as the rest of the class caught up.

Laura wasn't quite in the same boat.

"Need help?" I murmured to her after finishing the practice set in two minutes. It was excruciating to watch Laura jam her eraser into her paper again and again.

"Please!" she sighed.

I showed her how to do the problem, and just like that, something sparked between us. Dare I call it friendship?

At the end of class, Laura handed me a paper slip with writing on it. I read aloud, "1045 Baker Street, Richmond Hill. What's this?"

"My address," Laura said proudly. "Come over whenever you want. You got plans today after school?"

"Uh..."

I didn't know how to respond. Ever since the tuna sandwich incident, I hadn't hung out with anyone after school.

Struck by the depressing nature of that fact, I managed to nod my head and break out a smile. "I would love to come over!"

"Yay! Meet me outside the band room at 3."

4

The band room was a long, low building in the back of the school. But I heard it before I saw it.

The noise came from a gaggle of kids in front of the building. They all clutched some kind of instrument. As if holding babies, they fingered their glossy possessions while eagerly watching one student blow on a French horn.

"BLufdsfh." The fart noise again. Now I could see it came from the French horn, except if my memory held true, it wasn't supposed to sound like that.

"Angela!" Laura gave me a quick hug as she suddenly appeared. She was energetic and couldn't keep still. "I just need to get my violin from the band room and then we can go! Wanna come?" she said at rapid-fire speed.

"Violin?" I repeated stupidly.

Laura laughed, grabbed my hand, and dragged me inside.

My first thought was that there was a game of musical chairs going on inside the room. Then I recognized the rows of chairs arranged into layered half-moon shapes, reaching out to the furthest stretches of this clearly too-small room. Kids milled around, calling out to each other in voices barely audible above the overwhelming cloud of musical sound.

"Amazing, isn't it?" a voice behind me said.

I spun around and came face-to-face with a short, mousy man. His warm smile matched his gentle brown eyes and floppy hair.

"What, exactly?" I asked.

The man gestured to the room. "This. That so many contrasting individuals could learn to work together and move together as one to create beautiful music." He chuckled and held out his hand. "Mr. Crawley, the only music teacher at Clarity High."

"N-nice to meet you," I stammered, awkwardly shaking his hand.

"Have you ever played in an orchestra or band before?" Mr. Crawley asked.

I nodded and said, "I play the clarinet. But I've moved around so much in the last year that I just didn't join the school band for the last couple months."

Mr. Crawley clucked his tongue. "Every teenager should have music in their life," he insisted. "It's what grounds you, offers you comfort in stressful times-"

"Is Mr. Crawley going all philosophical on you?" Laura interrupted, appearing at my shoulder. She rolled her eyes and hiked her backpack up on her back. "Mr. Crawley, you're going to scare Angela away."

"Ah, I apologize," Mr. Crawley gave a mock bow. Laura and I both laughed. "Angela, whether or not you are moving again soon, I encourage you to join my band."

My insides itched to accept Mr. Crawley's invitation, but even as I nodded, I knew that I wasn't going to join his band. I most likely sucked at the clarinet by now since I hadn't practiced in months. And then there was the issue with Ma...

I thought about the last time I had played the clarinet in my own home and shuddered. Ma and music just did not mix.

5

She played the black and white keys with a graceful touch. White, black, white, black — the colors flashed before me, but from their movements came a beautiful sound.

"What is this?" I asked, entranced.

Laura smiled. "Für Elise," she said. "By Beethoven. Here, I'll teach you."

I had no idea what sheet music was. What eighth notes or bass clef meant. But following Laura's instruction, I somehow managed to learn the entire Für Elise song on the piano over the course of an hour. Pressing the keys felt magical; they were so accommodating, so responsive to my touch. Nothing before had ever been so easy to control.

"You really haven't ever played the piano before?" Laura asked after I played the last note, what I now knew to be an A.

"Yep. Never even touched one."

Laura turned toward me. She fixed her clear blue eyes on my mud-brown ones and said, simply, "Girl, you have a gift."

I laughed nervously and said, "Nah, I really don't."

Laura shook her head firmly. "Please tell me that you're going to join Mr. Crawley's band," she said. "We need you."

"Oh... oh no, I can't. I mean, I would love to, don't get me wrong. Music is great and all. But I can't." I stopped short once I realized I was starting to ramble.

Laura didn't miss a beat. "Why not?" she asked.

I opened my mouth to respond, but nothing came out. How was I supposed to explain my mother to this potential new friend? What would Laura think if she knew what Ma was like? I remembered what happened when classmates learned about Ma's fiery temper, how they turned away and avoided talking to me ever again.

But it was as if Laura could see inside my head. "You can tell me anything," she insisted. "I'm not going to judge you. Trust me, I'm the weirdo at school, so nothing you say could possibly surprise me." Although she said the last part sarcastically, there was something genuine in her voice that made me believe her.

"Ok, it's my mom," I sighed. "She, uh, well, she's kind of cranky. And when I play the clarinet, I mean, sometimes she's OK, but there have been some pretty messy episodes."

"Like what?"

After a few seconds of deliberation, I said, "Once, she burned all my sheet music. And my reeds. The day before this big winter concert."

Laura gasped. "Dear God, why?"

I shrugged. "She was in a bad mood and needed someone to take it out on, I guess. I was just there."

"Were you able to play in the concert?"

I laughed weakly. "Nobody would lend me a reed, so I had to just sit there and pretend to play."

"What? Not one person offered?" Laura exclaimed angrily.

"I was supposed to play a solo, but if I didn't, then it meant that another girl would get to play. And she was the popular one at that school, so I mean, yeah. I haven't played since then."

Laura clutched my hand suddenly and I jumped at the contact.

"That sucks so bad," she said sadly. Her eyes actually seemed to be filling with tears. Either Laura was an empathy addict or she was a natural actress. "I want to just beat those people up."

I shrugged again. It seemed like that was all I was good at.

"It's fine," I said. "I should probably just focus on my studies and helping out my mom anyway."

That statement clicked Laura into action. "Uh-uh, no," she said. "You're joining the school band. Whatever your mom needs can wait. Especially after how she treated you. This is more important."

Huh? I was mind-blown by what Laura said. Nothing could possibly be more important than fulfilling Ma's needs.

For the first time, I wondered if Laura was maybe a bad influence, one of those people that Ma warned me to never be around. But while Laura was certainly strong-willed, she didn't seem like a bad kid. Besides, I had told her about Ma's crazy antics, and she hadn't turned away. It was like she decided to defend me instead.

6

I kept replaying Laura's words in my head: "Whatever your mom needs can wait. This is more important." Her words swirled around in my mind as I walked home, as I cleaned up the table for dinner, as I rearranged the shoes, as Ma ranted at me about her day until my eardrums seemed to bleed.

I had a headache as I sat down for dinner: bland noodles with soggy veggies. Then I had a stomachache because Ma forced me to finish what must have been a gallon of broth.

That night, I had to pee literally six times. I counted because never before had my bladder undergone such an atrocity. On the sixth time, I stumbled to the bathroom to find Ma waiting for me outside it.

"I'm going to smack you if you don't stop," she hissed. "Stay in your room. You're being too loud."

It was so late — 3 AM — and we were both an incoherent mess.

"My bladder," I whispered. "About to explode. Ma, you fed me too much broth."

"Go to bed and be quiet," she snapped. Then she returned to her room.

"What kind of mother doesn't let her daughter pee?" I grumbled aloud to myself. What did she want me to do, just relieve myself on the carpet?

I reached for the door handle and twisted, but the door was locked. Unbelievable.

So I went outside and peed in the bushes. And that was when, with the prickly branches scratching up my bum and the night creatures hooting away, I decided that enough was enough. I was joining the school band

7

I guess I should talk about Mark.

On the days when I didn't follow Laura home like a sad puppy, I found refuge from Ma at school. Hidden in the back of the music room were some makeshift practice rooms with surprisingly good acoustics. I practiced for hours at a time, losing myself in the melody and the tricky bits of each song.

When all my energy was focused on this seemingly simple clarinet, it was like the rest of the world melted away. I emerged from the music room feeling refreshed and, for once, optimistic. Then it was time to hit the library.

That's where Mark comes in.

We first met because he was terrible at calculus. Actually, it seemed that everyone I interacted with was terrible at calculus.

In the middle of finding the derivative to question #23 on page 56, I heard someone clear their throat. Looking up, I fixed my eyes upon a lean, freckled boy with tousled brown hair. His eyes held this good-natured gleam.

"All the calculus textbooks are checked out right now. Mind if I share?" he asked.

It took me a couple seconds to nod. It had been so long since a boy last spoke to me. He sat by me, careful to keep our knees from touching, and then began to panic.

"The derivative must be, no, that's not right... Where is this 4 from? Is this the wrong lesson? I can't remember how to do this."

"Do you need help?" I asked finally.

I only had one problem left and hearing this guy's sighs was as painful as listening to a wounded animal moan. It seemed that calculus could truly inflict some pain.

"Please!" he said dramatically. His voice was light and pleasant, despite the obvious distress in it. "I'm totally lost."

I showed him how to do the problem... and then the next... and the next.

He's going to fail this class, I thought to myself. But of course, I didn't say that to him. Growth mindset, I suppose.

It took two hours. Two hours of dramatic gasping from Mark and patient explaining from my end, but he finally finished his homework. Mark offered to walk me home as a thank you.

God, the idea of Ma seeing a boy — and not even an Asian one — walking me home turned my insides to jelly.

"It's okay," I said. "I think I just need some time to think."

"At least let me make it up to you!" Mark insisted. "How about a coffee? Do you drink coffee?"

I shook my head. "My mom doesn't let me. She thinks caffeine is the devil's blood."

Mark was shocked. "No way, coffee is delicious!" he exclaimed. "Ok, I work at this coffee place on Barnhart Street, it's called Coffee Zone. Ever heard of it?"

I laughed. "I'm not allowed in those kinds of zones, so unfortunately, no."

Mark smiled and said, "All right, I'm going to bring you a cup tomorrow. No buts, please. You'll be addicted to caffeine forever after."

"That doesn't sound good."

Mark waved his hand airily. For someone who seemed to love caffeine, he sure seemed calm. In fact, there was something about his laidback attitude that made any lingering stress in my body melt away.

"Can you meet me here tomorrow, after school?" he asked.

I opened and closed my mouth several times like the confused fish I was. "Sure," I said finally. "Why not?"

8

I took my first sip of coffee the next day. Its rich, bold tones flooded my mouth, and I felt a sudden rush in my head within minutes of the first sip.

"Whoa!" I exclaimed. Some sort of weird buzzing was spreading to the tips of my fingers and toes. "This is way different than green tea."

Mark laughed. His eyes sparkled with excitement over my newfound love for the most basic of drinks. "I'm glad you like it! I get free drinks all the time, so I'll bring some different types for you to try, if you'd like."

It was impossible to turn down that offer. And so it went. For weeks and weeks, I headed to the library to sip on new coffee concoctions and help Mark with his math homework.

His need for math help continued. And I couldn't deny yet another free drink. My taste buds absorbed the zing of caramel macchiatos, the comfort of mochas, the richness of lattes, and the thrill of straight triple shot espressos.

It didn't matter that they impacted my sleep. For once, I didn't dread the break of day. I looked forward to getting out of bed.

I guess you could say that Mark and I were friends. It was so strange to me, to have a guy as a friend. Ma talked about boys as if they were poisonous creatures to avoid at all costs. And I was too self-conscious of my lack of girl charm — my so not-glowing skin, my too-small eyes, my not-glossy hair — to even try talking to them.

Yet here was Mark, bringing a nice change from the pettiness of girl drama. Willing to talk and share coffee with me. In between math problems, we talked about everything from politics to our shared love for golden retrievers. Finally, I could geek out about history with someone!

Don't get me wrong: Laura was a great friend, a spectacular friend. But Mark was the only friend I could debate healthcare policies with for hours on end. With him, there was no topic too small to discuss.

Of course, there was still turbulence at home. Ma seemed to rely on her morning rants as others do on morning yoga. A way to kick start the day. The littlest thing would set her off: a drop of orange juice spilled, the dry air in her bedroom, the simple act of clearing my throat.

But where her insults and jabs would normally hurt me, I just let them pass. My day would not be shaded by her fiery mood swings. I had too much to look forward to at school.

9

Usually, I'm pretty chill when it comes to high school teachers. They're hands-off and respectful of their students' hormonal mood swings. Best of all, they don't feel the need to inquire into their students' family lives.

And then there was Ms. Gladin. Oh, Ms. Gladin, so young, so sweet. Fresh out of New York University with colorful pencil skirts and stylish curls to boot. She taught us English and literature with plenty of poorly timed jokes and stretching breaks.

"It helps clear the mind," she insisted, as she led us through back stretches.

Although undeniably awkward, Ms. Gladin was genuinely nice and I loved literature. After class, I found myself drawn to her desk. I would ask for book recommendations and share with her what I was reading.

"Oh, I love *Anne of Green Gables!*" Ms. Gladin exclaimed when I showed her my latest find. Lucy Montgomery's series about a red-haired, daydream-prone orphan growing up in Canada had captured my heart. "She's such a delightful character."

"She's so relatable," I said, unable to hold back a smile at Ms. Gladin's excitement. "I wish I could have Anne as a sister, you know, just to have someone who understands."

Ms. Gladin leaned forward. The plastic gemstones on her necklace clinked together gently. "What do you mean?" she asked curiously.

"Well, Anne is an orphan and even when she lives with multiple families, she can't shake that off. Actually, even at Green Gables she'll never have that true connection with Marilla and Matthew that normal kids have. And, I don't know, maybe that's why she's so different from the other kids. Maybe she's not afraid to be herself because, deep down, she knows she will never fit in."

Ms. Gladin tilted her head, confused. "That's a beautiful observation, Angela. Forgive me if this is too personal... Are you an orphan?"

I laughed, realizing how my literary reflection must have sounded. "Oh, no, I'm not," I said. "I just... Well, my parents aren't the most warm or friendly towards me. Sometimes I feel like an orphan."

As the horror rose in Ms. Gladin's delicate face, I rushed to fix the damage.

"My parents are fine to me, don't worry," I said hastily. "I just, I wish that I could have a sibling. Someone who would understand."

"Like Anne," Ms. Gladin said, leaning back in her seat.

"Exactly, just like Anne."

Feeling uneasy at the troubled look on Ms. Gladin's face, I wished her a good day and scrambled out the door.

I probably shouldn't have told her all that, I thought. But somehow, I thought it would be fine.

How very wrong I was.

10

The next day, Ms. Gladin called me to her desk.

"I would like to have a chat with your parents," she said solemnly.

It was as if a train had barged into me.

"M-my parents?" I gasped. "Oh my gosh. Um... why?"

Ms. Gladin shrugged. "It's something I do with new students," she said. "Just to check in with their families, make sure that the student is adjusting well."

I couldn't believe this was happening.

"But, Ms. Gladin, you know me. You know that I'm adjusting well," I protested.

"Yes, well. I just want to make sure. Besides, it's a policy I have with new students."

"Ms. Gladin, this is your first year teaching."

With no other explanations at hand, Ms. Gladin simply handed me a slip to give to my parents. It was the kind of paper usually sent home when students were misbehaving.

Over dinner, I broke the news to Ma and Dad.

"My teacher wants to meet you," I said.

The noodle chewing stopped, and Ma looked up from her bowl.

"Why?" she asked.

"Uh…" I was stumped for words. "Well, it's a parent-teacher conference thing. She does it with all the new kids."

"She does it with all the new kids?" Ma asked again, as if making sure this wasn't a trap.

I nodded. "Yep, with all the new kids. She has been doing this for years now."

That tiny lie seemed to satisfy Ma. She nodded briskly and said, "I can do it this Friday, at 4 pm. Tell your teacher that."

"I can't do Friday." It was Dad, finally emerging from his own bowl of noodles and speaking for what must have been the first time that night.

Ma looked visibly annoyed. "Why not Friday?" she snapped.

Dad, steady and calm, said, "I'm working."

"At four?" Ma asked, confused.

Dad sighed and set down his chopsticks. "I've been working the cashier at Wong Kei for the past couple weeks."

I couldn't help but inwardly gasp. Dad had been holding a secret from Ma?

If Dad thought that the temptation of extra money would make the secret OK, he was terribly wrong. Ma's face immediately turned a bright, fiery red. Her eyebrows arched sky-high.

"Why didn't you tell me? All those late nights? Wong Kei? That place is no good. They always cheat me on their dumplings, never enough meat."

Her rants extended from the rational to the completely irrelevant. Dinner was twice as long that night. It's hard to eat with a screaming woman at the table. But by the end of the night, after Ma had slammed the bedroom door and stewed in her room for a good hour, she decided to forgive Dad.

"You bring the extra money straight home," she told Dad. "No drinking or wasting it on gambling."

As if Dad did any of those things.

Then she turned to me. "I will come alone," she said. "But you have to come with me."

Oh, gosh. The idea of sitting in on a parent-teacher conference made my stomach drop.

"It's only supposed to be you and the teacher," I tried to explain. "That way you can say anything."

"Do as I say!" Ma snapped.

She and I both knew that the reason she wanted me there was to serve as the mediator, in case she couldn't keep up with Ms. Gladin's well-spoken English. Language and cultural barriers were a touchy subject for my mom. Especially in a city where the only Asian restaurant was Wong Kei and it didn't meet her standards.

I approached Dad late that night. He was slumped on the couch, flicking through the TV channels. I sat down beside him. I felt the distance between us. And the fact that I didn't know what to talk about.

Finally, I asked, "Why did you hide the restaurant from Ma?"

Dad glanced at me, surprised that I was asking. "I didn't want to stress her out," he said.

"But she hates secrets. You must have known that hiding it from her would make things worse."

Dad scrunched up his face. He didn't like confrontation. He didn't like to talk much at all.

"Just focus on your studies. Don't worry about me and Ma," he said gruffly. And that was the end of that.

I sat alone in my room, feeling more like an orphan than ever before. If only Anne Shirley truly existed.

11

On Friday, I waited for an hour in Ms. Gladin's room for Ma to arrive. Normally, I would rush off to play my clarinet, but I was too stressed to think about music.

Ms. Gladin, cluelessly cheerful, babbled on about Toni Morrison.

Finally, Ma arrived. She wore a clean striped white shirt and sensible black pants. Her eyebrows were darker than normal. She looked tense and ready to bolt.

"Hi, Ms. Ma. I'm Ms. Gladin, Angela's English teacher," Ms. Gladin said sweetly, holding out her hand.

Ma shook it and gave a little dip of her head, saying, "Nice to meet you."

We both sat across from Ms. Gladin. I took a deep breath and tried to calm my nerves. So far, so good. No eruptions, screaming, or ranting yet.

"Ms. Ma, could you tell me a bit about Angela?" Ms. Gladin asked her first question.

My stomach clenched.

Ma looked taken aback. After a good minute, she finally responded, "She needs to study more."

Ms. Gladin laughed effortlessly. Against Ma's stone-cold expression, she was an overflowing vat of sparkly positivity. "I don't know if that's possible, actually," she said. "Angela studies so much already. She's my best student."

"Really?" Ma looked satisfied. The one thing she loved more than good food was compliments. I began to think that maybe this meeting wouldn't go so badly.

Ms. Gladin leaned forward now and took on a more serious tone.

"I'm really calling you in today, Ms. Ma, because I'm a bit concerned about Angela's home life," she said. Oh no. I felt my stomach clench again. "Is everything all right at home? Are there any issues with your husband or any family members?"

Silence. Ms. Gladin stared eagerly into Ma's narrowed eyes and waited. This was not good.

"Are you suggesting that I'm not taking good care of Angela?" Ma asked stiffly.

Ms. Gladin's eyes widened. "Oh, no, I'm not saying that," she said. "I just want to make sure that Angela is getting the support she needs at home."

Ma scoffed. "Don't tell me how to raise my daughter," she almost spat.

Just like that, our conversation hit rock bottom. Ms. Gladin's eyes widened almost in terror. I'm sure she had never faced such a sour person before.

"Have you had a kid? Do you even know what it's like to be a parent?"

"No, but—"

"Then don't tell me how to act! You don't know anything!" Ma hissed.

I waited in excruciating pain as Ma delivered several more of her finest insults. Many of them centered on Ms. Gladin's jewelry, which for some reason, Ma hated. Poor Ms. Gladin just sat there. She clearly had no idea how to respond to this angry, irrational lady. I didn't either.

Finally, Ma's steam wore off. She stood up and yanked me up by my elbow.

"I just want Angela to do well in school and get good grades," she snarled. "You just teach her and make sure she does that."

If there was one thing Ma hated above all else, it was disrespect. Unfortunately, what others saw as sensible, rational thinking, she saw as disrespect. So that was the end of that parent-teacher conference.

Ms. Gladin talked to me less after that. She seemed uneasy whenever I brought her new books. When I asked for book recommendations, she always mentioned some teacher meeting she had to run to.

It wasn't unexpected. The people in my life that Ma touched always seemed to disappear. I would too, except that I was sort of tied to Ma. Money and food, not to mention a bed to sleep in at night, meant that I just had to tolerate her behavior.

I was her daughter, after all.

12

If my days had some kind of consistency to them, it was because they revolved around one steady goal: to stay away from Ma.

My time at school or with my friends versus when I was at home was like night and day. When I was blowing into my clarinet, delighted at the glorious sounds that our band produced, or at Laura's house, where her mom fed us chicken salad sandwiches on homemade bread and I explored their piano, or even at the library, where I sat with Mark and discussed the Kennedys with him.

At all these places, I felt unbelievably free. My chest felt light. I smiled easily. I felt like a young girl.

Then I would come home, and everything darkened. My chest tightened and tears sprang to my eyes. My head ached from Ma's constant rants. I wanted to cry with frustration over Dad's passive silence. There was nobody to talk to, only insults to absorb and barbed questions to answer.

"What did you get on your math test?"

"97, Ma."

"English paper?"

"99, Ma."

"Chemistry exam?"

"92, Ma."

Then the raging started.

"92! That's terrible! You should be getting at least a 95! You think you'll get anywhere with a 92? Nobody will hire you. You won't get into college. You'll just be out on the streets. You should just go to a shelter now. You're pathetic. Go to your room. Stand there and don't move. Think about what a disgrace you are."

Standing there, for four hours at one point, I thought about what would happen if I tried to defend myself. To explain that science wasn't my strong suit, but that I loved history and English. To explain that 92 was, in fact, very good considering the class average was 78.

But fighting back would only lead to more punishments, more yelling, more goddamn standing.

13

The jellybeans looked ordinary. Sure, they were a bit of an unpleasant color, but hey, candy can be weird.

Laura and I found the beans on her desk in a little Claire's jewelry box. A note said, "Hey, you're awesome, enjoy these beans."

Everyone knew that Laura had a sweet tooth — she was always munching on Smarties or sucking on lollipops — so it wasn't a surprise that whoever was trying to impress her chose to do so through sugar.

Laura sniffed the beans and inspected them.

"Who do you think sent them?" I asked her.

She shrugged and popped one in her mouth.

"Argh!" Laura's eyes bulged. She spat the partially chewed, brown blob out. It flew across the room and hit Jack Davis in the back.

"What's wrong with them?" I asked, trying not to laugh.

Laura's face was stormy. "They're disgusting," she said. "I think they're one of those Harry Potter beans. The ones with the weird flavors."

Ah, it all made sense.

"What flavor is it?" I asked.

Laura wouldn't say. I finally took a bean and chewed off a little end. Ugh. Vomit flavor.

"Who gave these to you?" I asked her, and that's when I heard the sniggering.

Turning around, I spotted two of "the Sistas" laughing into their phones. They glanced in our direction several times, eyes bright with mirth.

"Careful, Laura," one of them said. She looked so glamorous, yet deadly with her words. "Too many jelly beans and you could get fat."

"They hate me," Laura told me later. She was gloomy the rest of the day.

"Why?" I asked.

I was surprised by how much the Sistas had affected Laura. The prank was cruel, and their remarks unwarranted, but they were just words. Laura had always seemed thick-skinned.

Laura sighed, running a hand through her hair. We were in her bedroom, which I considered to be one of the sunniest places that existed. Sunlight streamed in through a giant window, illuminating her light blue sheets and white furniture. It was a dream bedroom, just like Laura's life was dreamlike to me.

"I used to be friends with them," Laura said.

My jaw dropped.

"With the Sistas? I thought you hated them," I said.

Laura laughed. "I do hate them. But once upon a time, petty, shallow Laura sucked up to them and hung out with them every day."

I shook my head in disbelief. Bold, slightly cynical Laura was best friends with the Sistas? It was too hard to believe.

"OK, so what happened?" I asked.

"Well, I realized how stupid and shallow their lives were. All they cared about was their hair and how many Instagram followers they had, and yeah. It was just stupid."

I blinked twice. I didn't have social media, reason being that I didn't have a smartphone — thanks to Ma for that — but I knew all about it.

"That's it?" I said. "I don't get it. Why didn't you realize that at first?"

Laura shrugged. "I wanted to be like them. Those kinds of girls are so... glamorous and sparkly. They get all the guys. They seem so happy." She fixed her eyes on me.

"It's an illusion, you know. Their Instagram lives. It's all posed, all fake."

I laughed. "Laura, I don't even have Facebook. You don't have to worry about me."

Laura shrugged. "Look, I thought that I would be fine. But all those months of religiously, literally religiously, following girls' accounts, looking at their bikini pics and brunch trips — it took a toll."

She looked at me again, her eyes slightly watery. "That's why I love you, Angela," she confessed. I felt heat rise in my cheeks. "You're not like the other girls. You're not shallow or vain or obsessed with your appearance."

Taken aback, it took me several seconds to find words.

"I mean, I'm not totally satisfied with my appearance either. Like, I want to change parts of myself." As I said this, I realized it was not entirely true. There were often times when I wanted to change my *entire* self.

Laura tilted her head and asked, "What parts of yourself do you want to change?"

"Well, I wish I could dress better. I would love to own a skirt. To not just wear black, gray, or white all the time. And I wish I could get products to clear up my skin. I heard Katie talking about this new pimple cream. And, I don't know, I would love to get my nails done. Just girlish things, you know," I said sheepishly. Confessing all this felt so vain, almost forbidden.

Laura bounced up at my words. "Why don't you?" she asked, almost aggressively. "Those things are totally normal things to want, you know."

"Yeah, but my mom doesn't. She doesn't want me to do those things," I explained. I frowned at Laura, confused. "I don't get it. I thought you hated that kind of stuff."

"What kind of stuff?"

"Like caring about your appearance. Being vain."

"Oh, Angela," Laura looked at me sympathetically. "I'm sorry. I just meant don't base your entire self-worth on your appearance. That's the kind of thing that I hate. But wanting to look nice, to feel nice, that's not being vain. That's just self-care."

14

Laura met Mark and approved of him.

"How have I never met him before?" she exclaimed in delight.

The three of us formed, for lack of a better word, a squad. Laura could drive, so we would sometimes cram into her car after an exhausting day at school and hit the road. With the windows down and Rex Orange County blasting in our ears, I was in bliss. Mark always let me sit shotgun. He preferred to stretch out his legs in the back and make hilarious comments on teen arrogance.

"Did you see David flip me off?" he yelled over the music. "Wasn't even a good one."

I would stretch my head out the window, close my eyes, and feel the sun's warmth on my face. The wind whipped my short hair into a frenzy. Like beachy hair waves.

Horrified at my lack of "food culture," as Laura called it, we hit up nearly every non-Chinese restaurant in the area. I finally had poutine, a French dish of fries and gravy that Ma once physically restrained me from eating, Japanese curry, spaghetti and meatballs, and big, juicy burgers. Fries became my new obsession; my favorite were from McDonalds. And, of course, we all had plenty of coffee.

At first, my culinary forays had some unpleasant side effects. I was so used to eating bland, basically saltless foods that my stomach twisted and turned after each exploration. But it was worth it.

15

After one afternoon spent at Tim Hortons with Mark and Laura, I returned home feeling as if I were walking on starlight.

From the doormat, I could hear Ma and Dad talking. I crept into the living room.

"It still won't be enough."

It was Ma speaking.

"The aftercare is very long. The eye drops alone will cost hundreds."

What was going on?

Entering the kitchen, I found Ma and Dad seated around a pile of papers. The sheets were in a mess, which was surprising. Ma always wanted everything to be neat.

"I can take more hours at the restaurant," Dad said.

Ma nodded and rubbed her eyes. They still didn't notice that I was there. "There's an opening for a secretary position at a chiropractor place."

"Do you really think that will be OK, for your eyes?"

"What else am I supposed to do?" Ma turned her face up to the ceiling. It seemed like she was about to cry.

I cleared my throat. Ma's face snapped toward me. Dad slowly registered my presence.

"Why are you home so late?" Ma asked tensely.

I shifted my feet. "I was at Laura's. W-we were just cramming for a test."

Ma nodded. "Oh," was all she said.

I stood there for several seconds more. Awkward silence filled the room. Finally, I posed the question that had been burning into my mind.

"Are we going to do anything for my birthday, Ma?" I asked.

Ma's lips pressed together. "We'll go out for a nice dinner."

My heart sank. For the past four years, that had always been the case. A "nice" dinner out, at a typical Chinese restaurant where the waiters were rude and we couldn't order tofu (Ma believed soy was bad for the skin), followed by several hours of "free" TV time. Which was spent watching alone.

"I was wondering," I began tentatively, "if I could do something different this year? Like maybe have a birthday party?"

"A party?"

"You always did say that I could either have a party or a present," I reminded her.

It was true. Ever since I was ten, that had been the case. Party or big present (big present being a dinner).

With all the moving around, the party "option" hadn't really been an option. In order to have a party, you kind of need some guests. So, it had always been the present.

"Why do you want a party?" Ma asked. I could tell she wasn't fond of the idea.

"Well, I made some friends this year, and they're really nice. I think you would like them."

"Are they Chinese?"

"Um, no," I told her. I waited for her response, squirming.

Then Dad spoke up. "Why not, eh? A small party should be fine," Dad said. He smiled at me and said, "If they bring food, then it'll be even cheaper."

"Yeah!" I said, for once glad that Dad was so cheap. "See, Ma, my friends can bring food and that way we don't have to prepare anything. It'll be very low-key."

Ma sighed. "I'll have to clean the whole house, Angela, and what will your friends even do?" she said.

"Ma, the house is clean!" I protested. "We can just talk. And eat food."

Hope was dwindling within me. I knew it would be too much of a hassle. But then...

"Fine," Ma sighed. "But no more than two friends. And they can only stay for two hours."

"Yes! Thank you, Ma," I gasped.

Ha, I only had two friends, so that wouldn't be a problem. Maybe I should have thought of the fact that hosting a party would mean subjecting my friends to Ma's mood swings, but in that moment, I couldn't care less. Delight rose within me.

16

The party was set to be held on December 15, the day after school ended for Christmas break. My actual birthday is on December 14. Ma said hosting a party when school is in session is only what wannabe high school dropouts do. So, the birthday celebration would be one day late.

A grand total of two people were invited: Laura and Mark. I got away with inviting Mark by telling Ma that he was not only Laura's brother but also that he was gay.

"You did?" Mark gasped as Laura erupted in laughter. "Please tell me that you didn't."

"I'm sorry!" I said, spreading my hands apologetically. "My mom hates boys."

"Wait, and she's OK with gay people?" Laura asked. "I thought she was really conservative."

I shrugged. "My mom's not religious or anything. I think she doesn't fully understand what being gay means, anyway. The important thing is, Mark won't end up being a boyfriend."

"Oh, poor you, Mark," Laura joked.

Mark blushed beet-red and I laughed.

We were seated in Mark's coffee shop. We each had half-empty cups of coffee and croissant crumbs scattered on our plates. Caffeine drummed throughout my body.

"I'm so proud of you, Angela," Laura said. Her eyes were glimmering with mirth. "You've become so rebellious."

I shook my head furiously. "Oh, no. No way. Trust me, whatever my mom says goes."

"Should I be scared of your mom?" Mark asked. He looked a bit strange, a little furrow above his eyes. "She sounds awful."

"No, no, she's not," I exclaimed while Laura erupted in laughter. "No, seriously. I mean, she is cranky. But she's really thoughtful."

Laura pretended to choke on her latte. "Girl!" she cackled. "Remember when she burnt up your sheet music?"

"She what?" Mark's eyes bulged. "Tell me more."

I thought for a moment. So many stories to choose from… It was overwhelming.

"Ok, so my mom does this thing where she saves everything. And by everything, I mean every single last bread crust and noodle," I said. "So, once she ate half an orange and she wrapped the other half in plastic — oh yeah, that's the other thing. She thinks foil is dangerous so she only uses plastic. It's so weird. Anyway, so I notice that there's a little bit of mold on the orange, and I tell her so. She tells me to just cut that piece off and save the rest. So, I do what she tells me, but the next day, the mold has spread to the rest of the orange half."

Mark and Laura were both captivated. It struck me how strange my life must already sound to them, to two people whose families don't bother saving food scraps and only use Tupperware.

"OK, now the right thing to do would be to throw away the moldy orange, right?" I said. They nodded. "Right, OK, so that's what I did. And my mom went ballistic. She got so, so angry. Started yelling at me about how I was wasting food and how this wasn't my kitchen and how I have no respect for her."

Laura was laughing by now, but Mark was totally confused.

"Wait, wait, why was she so angry?" he asked. "Because that orange was moldy? Like, it would have made you guys sick."

"See, that's what a rational person would say," I said. "But my mom doesn't follow the normal human code of rationality. Oh no, it's as simple as this: if you don't do what she tells you to do, then you're disrespecting her. And disrespect is the worst crime you could possibly commit in her mind."

"Even if you're doing it for the right reasons and it makes sense?" Mark asked, even more confused than before.

"Bingo."

"Her mom is just *loco,* Mark," Laura said. "If she starts ranting at you, Angela told me not to even try defending yourself. Just take it like a rock."

Mark cringed. "God, your mom sounds awful, Angela. Maybe I'll pass on the party."

"No! Don't leave me alone!" Laura shrieked hysterically. "I can't be left with that tyrant."

I laughed, but felt a bit uneasy inside.

"I mean, it's only because she's tired and overworked," I heard myself explaining. "She's really not that bad."

Mark and Laura just stared at me blankly then burst out laughing.

"She loves me a lot," I said, more to myself than to them. It was true, after all.

17

During math class, Laura could not stop talking about the party. And about Mark.

"He totally likes you," she insisted for the third time. I just forced another laugh and shook my head.

"Where are you even getting that idea, Laura?"

"Please, he can't take your eyes off you. Why don't you just accept it? Barista boy is in love with you."

I thought about the dozens of hours spent at the library with Mark, us sitting closer and closer together as the weeks progressed. The trips to his coffee shop on Tuesdays and his insistence on making me a free drink.

"Laura, the chances of a boy liking me are less than my mom eating pizza."

Laura burst out in laughter, and then turned serious. Her mind jumped between subjects faster than flashes of lightning. "Wait, your mom has never eaten pizza before?"

"Nope. She only eats Chinese food."

"Oh my gosh," Laura seemed horrified, but her eyes were brimming with laughter. "Ok, I'm going to bring pizza to your party and your mom will have to try it. How can anyone not eat pizza?"

"She only likes bland food, so unless you plan to force feed her-,"

"I will do that! I'm serious!" Laura exclaimed.

"She'll probably throw up after, because she's not used to eating all that grease," I joked. Laura's face suddenly darkened. In the silence that followed, I heard some giggling from the seats near us. I turned and frowned at the sight of the Sistas wiggling their eyebrows at Laura mockingly. What was their problem?

"Careful Ching Chong," they said to me. "Laura might just do that, too." Their racist insult was so overused, it didn't even faze me. But Laura looked as if she really was going to puke.

"Come with me outside," she said darkly. Pulling me by the elbow, she rushed past a very confused Mrs. Crawfield and into the girls' bathroom.

"What's going on?" I asked, confused. "Is Mrs. Crawfield going to get mad?"

"No, don't worry about it," Laura said quickly. She took a deep, shaky breath. I had never seen her looking so nervous.

"What's wrong? You can tell me anything."

Laura nodded. "I know," she said. "That's why I'm going to tell you the truth. You wouldn't know this, since you weren't here last year, but I was bulimic."

Whoa. That was not what I was expecting. I didn't even know what to say. Laura nodded knowingly, seeing how shocked I was.

"I know, it seems so unbelievable, right? But it happened, and it was a horrible time in my life. It's over, though, it's in the past."

I couldn't believe this. Laura — happy, confident Laura — was bulimic? The thought of her forcing herself to vomit made me feel terribly sad.

"Does everybody know?" I asked.

Laura sighed and said, "Well, when I became bulimic I was friends with the Sistas. And they spy on all their friends because, well, they love, ahem, spilling the tea. So, they obviously found out and they told everyone. And then they decided that they didn't want to be friends with me anymore."

We both sat down on the hard-tiled floor. The florescent lights buzzed overhead. I stared at the smudged white wall, where people had written messages and notes in varying colors. Phone numbers in green and blue, unintelligible rants in pink, lips drawn in with lipstick.

"Why were you bulimic?" I finally asked.

Laura was quiet for a couple seconds. "I hated myself," she said finally. "I wanted to literally tear my skin off, to just get out of my body."

"Because of the way you looked?"

"Yes... and no." Laura wouldn't meet my eyes. "I just didn't like who I was. I thought that purging would change that. But it just made my teeth brown and made me hate myself even more." She sniffed and continued, "And then there was the whole Sistas thing. It made everything worse. They were always commenting on each other's bodies — on my body — and going on these crazy diets. And I was all obsessed with Instagram and Facebook, and everyone was posting pics of their bodies on there. It was just a mess."

She looked up and met me with wet blue eyes, eyes that glimmered above the sparkling tears splashed on her face.

"The worst part of all, was that I wanted control, and I thought that purging would give me that," she whispered. "Which is crazy, right? If you're bulimic, then you have no control. It's the complete opposite."

"So, it was like a coping mechanism?" I asked.

She nodded, and I reached out to put my arms around her. Hugging Laura, resting my chin on top of her head, I tried to imagine how she must have felt. Scared and alone, feeling like life was pressing down on her with such a weight that she wanted to climb out of her body.

The scary thing was, that was exactly how I felt, too.

18

One day, Mr. Crawley called me into his office after band practice. I fidgeted with my clarinet as he rifled through his filing cabinet for something.

"Ah, here it is," he said, emerging with a manila folder. "The jackpot."

He handed the folder to me, and I opened it to find notes. A lot of notes. Frenzied sixteenth-notes with high G sharps and some nasty looking trills.

"What is this?" I asked.

"Your solo," he responded.

My jaw dropped.

"Mr. Crawley, I don't think... I'm not ready—" I sputtered, but he cut me off.

"Angela, you have shown yourself to be an extremely determined, hard-working, and passionate musician," he said plainly. "I would like to promote you to be first chair."

Silence. I was speechless. Words... Where were my words?

"I know that you practice more than anyone in the band, heck, in the entire music department," Mr. Crawley said with a wide grin. "I've seen you practicing after school."

"Mr. Crawley," I finally said, when my voice had returned to me. "I think you must be mistaken. I'm not the best. I'm only, I mean, I may be decent, but only because, as you said, I practice so much. There are so many better players. I mean, Jack, his trills are sick. And Margaret is so—"

"Angela," Mr. Crawley interrupted. "I want my first-chair violinist to be someone who has the drive and work ethic to improve upon their work. No matter how good he or she may be."

I stuttered for several seconds, trying to think of how to respond. There was no way I could do this. Absolutely no way.

"I'm sorry," I said weakly. "But I can't be first chair. I just can't. I'm not ready."

Mr. Crawley gazed at me steadily for several seconds. Then he sighed and turned away.

"I guess Jack will just stay as first chair for now, then. Too bad, I would have liked to hear you perform that solo," he said. Then, when I tried to hand him back the sheet music, he shook his head. "Keep the music. Play it for fun at home. Or toss it. Whatever gives you more comfort."

19

I have a quote from this book that I love. It says, "You'll understand why storms are named after people." It's from *The Beautiful and Damned* by F. Scott Fitzgerald.

I would love to think that I'm the Beautiful, but let's be real. I'm the Damned. For when I came home that Tuesday night, a storm was waiting for me.

The house was silent. No TV commercials or casual chatter. It was late, almost 9 pm, the latest I had stayed out so far.

I was caught off guard. I should have known to be warier, but I was on a musical high, drunk on Chopin's chords and Laura's good energy.

Ma was waiting for me in the living room. Her face was ashen white. Her lips had never been more tightly pressed together.

"Hi Ma!" I chirped, throwing my backpack on the couch. "Where's Dad?"

"He's not here." Ma said. Her voice, chillingly sharp, immediately sent knives down my spine.

"What happened?" I asked tentatively.

"What happened?" Ma raised her eyebrows. Her voice seemed to climb an octave. "What happened? What happened is that your father is an uncontrollable, selfish, bastard of a man!"

Ma was shrieking now. The eye of the tornado had hit home. And off she went.

This was the worst rant of all. I could barely understand what Ma was saying, she was speaking so fast. From the fragments of "that other woman" and "always at the restaurant," I gradually pieced together the puzzle.

Dad was having an affair with Betsy? The owner of the Wong Kei restaurant? For... two months now? It was unimaginable. Yet here was Ma right in front of me, screaming that this was the truth.

My thoughts were racing. How could this be? There's no way that Dad would ever cheat on Ma. Betsy was married. She had kids.

Dad was married, too. He had me. He had a kid, too. He wouldn't do this to me. Not Dad.

"Ma!" I pleaded. "Are you sure that Dad did this? He's not that kind of person—"

"You mean the kind of person who doesn't care about his own family?" Ma screamed. "Of course, he is. Just like you!"

"Just like me? What? I don't understand!"

Oh, how her anger had turned so quickly to me!

"You are a useless daughter. Coming home at midnight, kissing up to those white families—"

"Ma!" I protested. "I don't come home at midnight. And I'm not kissing up—"

I stopped short. Had I ever talked back before? Attempted to defend myself? Not for a long time. It was forbidden under this roof. And Ma's face said it all. I felt something like fear ooze throughout my body.

"Xià guì!" she spat in Chinese. "Kneel down."

So I did.

With my knees sinking into that grubby carpet, the rage of my mother thundering down, I felt tears trickle down my cheeks. In that moment, I was a pitiful waterfall. Even my crying was weak. But my mother, she was a terrific hurricane.

"You are pathetic. You are worthless. You are useless. The worst daughter. The daughter who brings shame to the family." Every insult my mother could imagine spewed from her lips.

Looking back, I have to wonder... Did she truly mean what she said? Or was this just how she released years of pent-up anger?

Anger that first started at a young age, from a difficult childhood where half her siblings died of illness. Then, maybe it spiraled out of control from working in factories, gaining strength with every calloused finger and sour manager. From poor wages and long hours, from nights spent alone in unheated apartments.

Maybe that anger calmed a bit when she met Dad. Maybe falling in love (was it even love, or just financial necessity?) beat down her cynicism. But then as the years continued, with each move and each new job in another desolate library, as the money never came and it never got easier, that anger grew again.

This time, in full force in adulthood, it was hard and cold, like steel. There was no room for hope in that anger.

20

Ma disappeared for days. I didn't know where she went, and the only reason I didn't call the police was because she left a note: "Don't call the police."

Would she come back?

I asked myself this question dozens of times. The house was strangely quiet without her presence. No one was constantly sweeping up the hairs in the bathroom, or ranting about other humans, or humming as they did the dishes.

I sat at dinner alone with Dad every night. We always had takeout from the restaurant he worked at and where, apparently, he was having an affair with the owner. I didn't know if I should say anything. I guess part of me was hoping that Ma was mistaken. If I didn't confront Dad, then it would mean that his betrayal wasn't true.

"Is there something wrong with Ma's eyes, Dad?" I asked him over potstickers.

He took his time to chew and swallow before answering.

"Her eyes are very bad," he said.

"How bad?" I asked, thinking that all those long nights at the library must be getting to her.

"She's going blind in her right eye."

I was speechless. "Oh," was all I could manage to get out, and then we were silent. Him eating, me sitting in shock.

"Why didn't Ma tell me?" I asked him.

"She didn't want to worry you."

"Was it supposed to be a secret?"

Dad paused before answering. "Yes."

I nodded, trying my best to absorb the information. "Thanks for telling me, Dad," I said.

Silence once more.

I couldn't believe this. I thought of how much Ma loved to read. For the past several weeks, she hadn't been reading as much anymore. In fact, I couldn't remember the last time I saw Ma bring home a new book.

"Dad," I said. I needed to know. "Did you really cheat on Ma?"

He didn't respond for what seemed like a lifetime. He just stared at the same spot on the table, his eyes blank and lifeless.

"Your ma doesn't want me to say anything about that," he said finally.

My heart nearly caught in my throat. I wanted to cry.

"So, you did," I challenged him. "You cheated on Ma with that woman."

"Your ma doesn't want me to say anything," Dad said.

"How could you do that to our family?"

"Look." Something came into Dad's eyes, something I had never seen before. "Your ma is not the perfect lady, either. She yells at me, she nags at me. She tells me I'm fat, that I'm a loser. She's not perfect, either."

"I know, I know," I said.

And we both went back to staring at different spots on the table, lost in our thoughts. I noticed Dad's hands clenched together tight, his knuckles white.

I realized what had entered his eyes. It was anger. Anger and resentment and bitterness. Anger toward our lack of money, toward his complex situation. Toward Ma, for not loving him the way she should. And now he had gone and stabbed her in the back.

My throat tightened up more. I had to leave the table.

Curled up on my bed, I felt tears fall hot and fast across my face. I didn't want to be like my dad, so overcome with resentment that he turned to hurting other people. And I didn't want to be like I was now, so pitiful and weak that I couldn't stand up for myself.

Where was the middle ground? Was it even possible to find it with Ma in my life? Was it possible to find myself, a version of Angela that wasn't corrupted or molded by Ma's influence?

21

When Ma came home a week later, it was at 3 am. I woke up to the shuffle of her slippers and crept out into the hallway.

There she was, looking so small and delicate in a baggy sweater and too-large jeans. In just one week, she had lost so much weight.

"Ma," I whispered. "Are you OK?"

She turned towards me. Her eyes looked sunken, her cheeks hollow. "No," she said simply. "I'm not."

We stood there in silence for several moments. It struck me that, for once, Ma was not dealing with her anger by ranting. It was kind of scary. Did she not have the energy to do even that?

"I missed your birthday," she said.

"Oh, yeah. It's OK."

"Did you have your party?"

"No, I canceled it." I tried to make it sound like it wasn't a big deal. Ma always said that I was asking for too much.

Indeed, Ma didn't seem concerned. She told me that she needed some tea. She sat down in the kitchen chair, absolutely spent.

I made her tea, steeping the teabag just as she liked, with the lid on top of the cup. Then I sat down with her and watched her drink the tea.

Only after the cup was empty did Ma speak. "I wanted better for you," she said huskily. I had never seen her this tired before. "I wanted you to have a good childhood and a good life."

"Ma, I do have a good life."

"No, you don't. I failed you. You won't amount to anything, at this rate. We shouldn't have moved around so much. Then maybe you could have gone to private school."

How to tell her that the moving was difficult, yes, but not the worst thing? How to explain to my own mother that it was her, her screaming and her stinging insults, that truly failed me? Even now, she couldn't help but tell me how worthless I was.

"I'm trying, Ma," I said, trying not to cry. "I just want to make you happy."

"Angela," Ma took a deep breath, closing her eyes. "Never settle for less. You promise me that you will never settle for less. Marry a good man, one who will work hard. Find a good job and a good home. Maybe one day you can even buy your own piano."

She tried to speak more but seemed too fatigued. I watched as Ma got up to make more tea and thought about her words. For a moment, I could almost see into this insane woman's mind. I could see how she wanted the best for me in a world that had been so cruel to her.

She was so different from my classmates' moms. But they didn't have to work in a factory at age five.

That night — or morning, I should say — I drank tea with Ma and caught her up on my school and activities. She was surprisingly interested in my clarinet and love for the piano. I didn't bother asking her to come to a concert, for she had never come to any of them before. Just having a pleasant conversation and gossiping about our neighbors was enough.

22

"God, I hate this!" Laura cried.

With a scream, she grabbed her backpack and hurled it into the air. It flew two feet before skidding to a stop.

Curled over the toilet, the gentle dripping of the broken faucet in the background, Laura looked like a mess. Her blonde hair hung in strands over her tear-streaked face. Her fists banged against the stall wall in frustration.

"I told myself I wouldn't! I wouldn't, I wouldn't! I freakin' hate myself," she wailed.

I stood there, dumbstruck, wanting to help but having no clue as to how I could.

It was after school, on a Wednesday. I had found a gaggle of girls hanging outside the bathroom. Some were laughing and others looked horrified. Pushing my way in, I found Laura. Or the past version of Laura, the one that she had sworn was gone forever.

"I suck. I literally... Why do I do this? Why?" Laura cried.

"Why do you do this?" I asked softly.

Both of us knew that Laura had told me the answer to this question before. It was pointless to ask, but I asked nonetheless. I was dying to know why she would hurt herself like this.

"Because I hate myself," Laura growled. "But I just hate myself even more now. God, I want to stop. I-I literally. I hate myself. Why do I do this?"

I stood there for a good minute, watching Laura do anything but keep still. She had worked herself into a frenzy, her face growing red as she banged her feet against the floor and cried out in frustration, "I hate myself. I suck. Why do I do this?" Over and over.

It was unbearable to see my friend in pain. This was the side of her disorder that I never saw. Up until now I had only been given glimpses into what it was like. Laura had made it seem like her disorder, and her thoughts, were under control. Now, it was clear she was crumbling from within.

I went to the sink and pulled out some paper towels. After wetting them, I handed them to Laura so she could wipe the vomit from her chin.

"You're going to get better," I told Laura as confidently as I could.

She glared up at me, her blue eyes now dark and stormy. "What do you know?" she spat.

Her words — her vicious tone — stung. She was almost unrecognizable, this disheveled, angry girl.

"You can't even take care of yourself," Laura hissed. "It's pathetic. And you're telling me that you know, ha, that you just know I'm going to get better? Give me a break."

"What are you even talking about?" I said. It felt so strange to have to be defending myself against Laura, against my best friend. It was as if this scene was happening to someone else, and I was observing from above. "I think you need to just rest right now."

"You are pathetic," Laura said boldly. Just like that, something inside me shattered. "Don't tell me you aren't ashamed of your weirdness, always stumbling around, all pitiful and small. You can't do anything yourself. It's like you're a toddler."

Heat rose to my face. I felt something drumming within me, rising and growing with every heartbeat. I was done. I had to deal with Ma insulting me at home. Having more knives shoved into what little dignity I still had was just too much.

"What do you want?" I screamed. I was so tired, mind and body both spent. Yet I was also full of frustration, the type that could only explode, not leak out slowly. "I don't know how to make you happy, Laura."

"Don't worry about making *me* happy," Laura snapped. "I want *you* to be happy, to stick up for yourself, to do what makes you smile."

What was she even saying? "If this is about my mom again, I told you. Arguing with her just makes everything worse," I snapped.

"No!" Laura shrieked. She's crazy, I thought to myself. We're crazy. She whispered fiercely, "I want *you* to be selfish. I want you to paint your nails, to do a face mask. Buy sheet music because you want to, go on that date because you want to. Stop bending over for everyone but yourself."

Laura was crying by then. In that moment, I felt something crackle in my throat. I realized I was crying.

"I don't know how," I whispered, for that was all I could manage. Just like that, all the anger evaporated from my body. I was left an empty shell, having nothing left to offer. "I'm so tired, Laura. And I'm scared of my Mom. I want to please her, but I don't know how to do that."

"Angela," Laura sniffled. Distraught, disorientated, she seemed to retain this glimmering touch of sanity. "You weren't put on this earth to please your Mom, or anyone for that matter."

It seemed so obvious, but that simple statement shook me to the core.

23

After Laura calmed down, and we both stopped crying, she put eyeliner on both of us. I gazed at my new eyes in the mirror, eyes that had depth and mystery, and found that I actually liked them. From then on, I was hooked on eyeliner. It made me feel more powerful.

Then I went to the music room. Somehow, I knew Mr. Crawley would be there.

Sure enough, he was sitting in his office, composing music. It was as if he knew that something momentous would happen that day. That a best friend would break reality to me and tell me what seemed obvious to others but invisible to me. That I would decide to stop victimizing myself and take the opportunities given to me. That I would stop hiding in fear.

"I would like to accept your offer of first-chair violinist," I said, in a slightly wavering voice.

Mr. Crawley peered at me over bronze-rimmed spectacles.

"Are you sure?" he asked.

I nodded and said, "I've never been more sure of anything."

Mr. Crawley's face broke into a wide smile. "I knew you had it in you," he said. "Do you still have the sheet music for the solo I assigned you?"

"Yep. I've actually played it a few times."

"Excellent." He was beaming. Just as I was about to leave, he said one last thing: "Remember to bow, after."

24

We messed up. So many times. But as Mr. Crawley said, the audience only knows what we show. And what we showed were beaming faces, good spirits, and zeal for the music we were playing. I felt drunk on the good energy around me, riding on a musical high.

It was only at the end, when I stood up to bow as Mr. Crawley introduced me as the new first-violinist and the soloist of the night, that I realized Ma was in the audience. She was smiling. Her hands were clasped together in excitement.

Ma was happy. Whether happy for the fact that I was happy or because I was first-chair–the best, as she would later say—I didn't know. But it did not matter.

I took a bow. And for once, it wasn't towards Ma. It wasn't even for the crowd.

It was, selfishly and indulgently, for me.

About The Author

Caroline is 17 years old and lives in San Francisco, California. She loves nonfiction writing and gains inspiration from memoirists like Frank McCourt and Mary Karr. When she is not reading or writing, Caroline loves to run, hike, bake, and drink too much coffee. She hopes to continue improving her writing and sharing her work with others as she enters into college.

About The Publisher

Story Shares is a nonprofit focused on supporting the millions of teens and adults who struggle with reading by creating a new shelf in the library specifically for them. The ever-growing collection features content that is compelling and culturally relevant for teens and adults, yet still readable at a range of lower reading levels.

Story Shares generates content by engaging deeply with writers, bringing together a community to create this new kind of book. With more intriguing and approachable stories to choose from, the teens and adults who have fallen behind are improving their skills and beginning to discover the joy of reading. For more information, visit storyshares.org.

Easy to Read. Hard to Put Down.

Angela

www.ingramcontent.com/pod-product-compliance
Lightning Source LLC
Chambersburg PA
CBHW072231190626
46809CB00017B/1693